EMMA

JANE AUSTEN

Borrow-a-Book

Y4

www.realreads.co.uk

Retold by Gill Tavner
Illustrated by Ann Kronheimer

Published by Real Reads Ltd
Stroud, Gloucestershire, UK
www.realreads.co.uk

First published in 2008
Reprinted 2013, 2014, 2015, 2017

ISBN 978-1-906230-10-4

Printed in China by Imago Ltd
Designed by Lucy Guenot
Typeset by Bookcraft Ltd, Stroud, Gloucestershire

CONTENTS

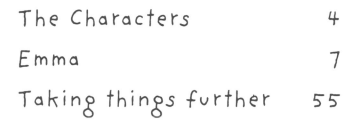

THE CHARACTERS

Emma Woodhouse

Emma is beautiful, clever and rich. Does she truly understand other people's hearts? Does she even understand her own?

Mr Woodhouse

Emma's frail father is afraid of wedding cake and afraid of change. Does he really have anything to fear?

Harriet Smith

Harriet is seventeen, pretty, and easily led. Will her friendship with Emma bring her happiness? How many men can a girl love in one year?

Mr Elton

The gallant Mr Elton seems keen
to marry. Can Emma find him
the right wife?

Mr Knightley

Emma's friend and neighbour is
a perfect gentleman. Can he undo
the damage caused by her father's
indulgence? Can he escape her
matchmaking schemes?

Jane Fairfax

Jane Fairfax is beautiful, talented
and honest. Or is she? Why
doesn't Emma like her? Is her
reserved nature hiding a secret?

Frank Churchill

Frank is a lively young gentleman whom
Emma quickly likes. Why doesn't Mr
Knightley like him? Does he really travel
to London just for a haircut?

My dear sister Cassandra,

Thank you for your entertaining letter. I cannot reply at length as I am busy with my next novel, 'Emma'. Instead of letters, I will send you chapters as I write them. I hope you enjoy it. The plot will present you with a series of puzzles, but I must warn you that you might guess twenty things without guessing correctly.

I wonder what you will think of Emma herself? I think perhaps I have created a heroine whom no one but myself will much like. Let me know what you think.

Affectionately,

Jane

EMMA

'Please don't eat too much wedding cake, my
dear,' cautioned the frail Mr Woodhouse. 'It
is very bad for the stomach. Indeed, weddings
in general are very bad for the health. They
always mean change, and change is always so
troublesome.'

'Dearest father,' soothed Emma, 'you must
surely agree that Mr and Mrs Weston's marriage
promises them both great happiness.'

'But Emma, how will you bear the loss of your
governess's company now that she has married?'

Mr Knightley, a trusted and respected family
friend and neighbour, rescued Emma from
this line of conversation. 'I am sure Emma has
sufficient liveliness of spirit to occupy her days,'
he assured Mr Woodhouse, accepting a second
piece of cake from Emma.

'Thank you, Mr Knightley,' smiled Emma.
'Besides, I congratulate myself upon making this
match. I always thought Mr Weston would be

a most suitable husband for Miss Taylor. Having experienced such success, I shall now fill my hours making similar matches for our other friends.'

'Please leave me out of such foolish schemes,' frowned Mr Knightley.

'Avoid all such schemes, my dear,' said an alarmed Mr Woodhouse. 'We do not want any more marriages.'

'Don't worry, father, I shall not make matches for myself or for Mr Knightley, so you need not fear too much change.' Mr Knightley was such a regular and valued visitor at Hartfield that any change in his situation would indeed be a blow to Mr Woodhouse.

Mr Knightley smiled. 'I am pleased that you will kindly leave me to find my own happiness, Emma.' With a sterner, more concerned look, he drew Emma away from her father's hearing. Mr Knightley, who had known Emma all her life, was one of the few people who could see faults in her, and the only one who ever told her of them. 'Emma, Mr and Mrs Weston found each other without your help.

You cannot claim success. You should not try matchmaking. Meddling in other people's affairs can only do harm.'

They rejoined Emma's father, who immediately raised the same matter. 'Mr Knightley, Emma thinks that Mr Elton would be made happy by a good wife. She is generally right about such things. Is there any danger of his marrying?'

Mr Knightley assured Mr Woodhouse that Mr Elton, the eligible new vicar, was, at present at least, free from danger.

'Leave Mr Elton to find his own wife,' he warned Emma quietly before turning his full attention to the wedding cake, a look of displeasure on his face.

So, dear Cassandra, having acquired a taste for matchmaking, Emma plans to do more. Will she ignore Mr Knightley's warning?

Beautiful, rich and clever, Emma lived alone with her father in their magnificent home, Hartfield. Their friendliness, wealth and status ensured them many friends in the nearby village of Highbury. Emma had everything she needed, except for one thing. Following the early death of her mother, and particularly now after her governess's wedding, she lacked female company.

Several lonely weeks after the Westons' wedding, Emma was introduced to a sweet, pretty seventeen-year-old girl called Harriet Smith. Not knowing who her parents were, Harriet had grown up in a local boarding school, where her good nature endeared her to everyone. Harriet spent much of her free time with a family of good friends, called the Martins. Harriet immediately interested Emma.

Perhaps Emma simply wanted a new friend, or perhaps she wanted a new matchmaking project. Maybe it was both. Can we blame Emma if she wanted the challenge of finding a husband for Harriet? After all, a wealthy husband would improve Harriet's status and give her the lifelong security rarely achieved by girls in her situation. In finding her a husband, Emma felt sure she would be doing her a great service.

Emma invited Harriet to Hartfield with increasing regularity. Having been adored, constantly praised, and quite spoilt by her father, Emma was not looking for a friend whose talents might rival her own. Humble, grateful, and easily persuaded, Harriet was Emma's ideal companion. Although not able to match Emma's lively mind, Harriet provided her with enough interest to make her company enjoyable.

Emma quickly noticed that Harriet's conversation frequently turned to her friends, the Martins. Knowing that the Martins' farm was on Mr Knightley's land, and that Mr Knightley had great respect for the family, Emma was intrigued to find out more about them.

Walking into Highbury one afternoon, Emma and Harriet happened to meet the son of the family, Mr Robert Martin. Emma was surprised to see Harriet blushing, and in a flutter of spirits as Robert Martin approached.

Watching carefully, Emma noted that they talked to each other with shy smiles and considerable affection.

'Oh, Miss Woodhouse!' gasped Harriet, her face glowing as she ran back to Emma's side. 'How lucky we should meet him. He was so pleased to see me. Miss Woodhouse, do you like him? Don't you think him very handsome?'

'For a common farmer,' replied Emma, suddenly aware of the danger, 'he is pleasant enough, although certainly not handsome. Surely after meeting a true gentleman such as Mr Elton, you must see that Mr Martin lacks gentility and seems a little clownish.'

Poor Harriet's smile vanished. 'Well, of course he isn't as fine as Mr Elton or Mr Knightley, but they are such refined gentlemen.'

Emma was a little affronted that Harriet should consider the somewhat vain Mr Elton to be Mr Knightley's equal. She replied, 'Even without making the comparison, Mr Martin is awkward and uncouth.'

'Oh,' said Harriet quietly. 'Is he? Well, you must be right.'

Harriet's spirits seemed low as they walked back to Hartfield, but an idea of Emma's lifted them a little.

'Let us invite Mr Elton to supper tomorrow,' she suggested. 'You will surely see that his gentlemanly manner is so much superior to the roughness of Robert Martin.'

Dear Cassandra, are you surprised that Emma is concerned by this encounter with Robert Martin? Has she already made her own plans for Harriet? Do you believe that she truly has her friend's best interests at heart?

The next day dawned bright and sunny. Mr Elton was delighted to accept an invitation to supper from the charming Emma Woodhouse, and Emma and Harriet were delighted at his acceptance. However, danger arrived with the morning post – danger in the form of a marriage proposal to Harriet from Robert Martin. Emma watched with concern as a blushing, trembling Harriet read it. 'Pray, read this, Miss Woodhouse,' she said as she offered the letter.

Emma was not sorry to be asked. She had to admit to herself that it was a sensible letter. The grammar was faultless, and the feelings expressed were sensitive and genuine.

'Well?' said Harriet anxiously. 'What shall I do?'

'What shall you do? The man is determined to marry well, but can he not see how far above him you have risen since your friendship with me? My dear Harriet, I shall not give you any advice, but do make sure that you let him down gently.'

'You think that I ought to refuse him?' Harriet whispered.

'You must decide that for yourself, Harriet. Remember, we have Mr Elton's visit to look forward to once the letter is written.'

Now, dear sister, you are becoming acquainted with our friends. Do you like Emma? Is she a good friend to Harriet? Let's see what Mr Knightley has to say.

That same afternoon, an angry and agitated Mr Knightley paced around the Hartfield drawing room. 'Emma, you have been no friend to Harriet! Robert Martin is an intelligent gentleman farmer. She cannot hope for a better match.' Emma tried to look unconcerned, but disliked having Mr Knightley's opinion so strongly against her.

'I believe your friendship with Harriet to be a foolish one. You will fill her head with nonsense, and your matchmaking will do her great harm.' Mr Knightley looked at Emma searchingly.

'If Mr Elton is your idea of a suitable match, you will be disappointed. He is more likely to marry for money than for love. Harriet will not interest him. Good day to you.'

Dear sister, I am keen to cause some mischief.

Mr Elton was a handsome, charming young vicar. Always a welcome guest at Mr Woodhouse's supper table, this evening he was even more welcome than usual.

In his company Harriet behaved perfectly. Following Emma's advice, she said very little and looked very pretty. Emma thought that Mr Elton showed all the early signs of falling in love.

Mr Elton praised Emma as they watched Harriet talking to Mr Woodhouse. 'You have added many attractions to Miss Smith,' he said. 'She was pretty before she came to you, but you have added qualities that nature did not provide.'

'I am glad if I have been useful, but really
there was little to add.'

'If I might contradict a lady,' said Mr Elton
gallantly, 'I must argue that you have passed many
of your own fine qualities on to your friend.'
Mr Elton's sighing admiration surprised even
Emma. Even though she had planned the match,
she was astonished at the speed of his growing
affection. Encouraged, she had an idea. 'Mr

Elton, would not it be wonderful to have a portrait of Harriet? I should like to paint her myself. Would not that be an exquisite possession?'

'It would be a delight!' exclaimed Mr Elton. 'Let me encourage you, Miss Woodhouse, to exercise your talent in honour of your friend. It would indeed be an exquisite possession.'

Although Emma was pleased by his enthusiasm, the formality of his speeches made her want to giggle. She turned away.

So, Cassandra, the matter was decided. Emma was to bring the two together again the following week. Mr Elton would have every opportunity to gaze at Harriet whilst Emma painted the picture. Can you imagine the mischief I have in mind?

The portrait sessions went well. Harriet sat, blushing and pretty, while Emma painted and Mr Elton sighed over the beauty of the painting. Emma admired his subtlety; it would perhaps seem too forward were he to praise Harriet's beauty directly. When the picture was finished, he offered to take it away to be framed.

'My dear Harriet, I do believe he is in love with you already,' said Emma happily.

Easily persuaded of the superiority of Mr Elton's manners over those of Mr Martin, Harriet smiled.

'Oh, Miss Woodhouse, if it hadn't been for you I should never have considered myself worthy of Mr Elton.'

Emma sensed imminent success. Mr Knightley would have to admit his error.

A few days later, the recently married Mr and Mrs Weston held a dinner party at their home. With great excitement, Mr Weston announced that his son Frank, from a previous marriage, was soon to pay a visit. After his mother's death, Frank Churchill had been raised by a wealthy aunt in another county. Although he had a reputation for being a fine young man, he had never honoured Highbury with a visit. The prospect of meeting him for the first time sparked everybody's curiosity. Emma was particularly keen to meet him. With adequate wealth of her own and a reluctance to leave her invalid father, Emma had no intention of marrying. However, she felt that if she were ever to change her mind, Frank would be her ideal match in age, character and wealth.

Eager to hear more about Frank from Mrs Weston, Emma was frustrated to find Mr Elton constantly at her side. She managed only a brief conversation with her former governess, and an even shorter one with Mr Knightley. 'Mr Elton appears to have grown particularly attentive towards you lately,' he commented, smiling. Emma felt uncomfortable.

At the end of the evening Mr Elton contrived to share a carriage home with Emma. 'Perhaps he wants to ask me about Harriet,' she hoped. However, shining with wine and optimism, Mr Elton had other ideas. As soon as the journey started, he seized Emma's hand and confessed his strong affection, his unequalled love. In short, he told her that he would die if she refused him.

'Mr Elton,' replied Emma in displeasure,
'I am far from being grateful. How can you be so
inconstant? What about your love for Harriet Smith?'

'Harriet Smith?' Mr Elton seemed offended.
'Who can care whether Harriet Smith lives or dies
when the charming Miss Woodhouse is nearby?'

*Oh dear. Did Mr Elton's proposal surprise you,
Cassandra, or had you seen the warning signs? I will
leave you to imagine the awkward, angry silence that
accompanied the rest of the journey. I will also leave
you to imagine Emma's feelings as she reluctantly told
Harriet the next morning where Mr Elton's affections
lay, and watched Harriet's tears flow. Poor Harriet.
How long would it take her to recover from such
heartbreak?*

Before Frank Churchill's long-awaited visit,
Highbury received another visitor. Jane Fairfax was
the niece of Miss Bates, a friendly spinster from

the village who had fallen upon hard times. Jane had had the good fortune to be raised by wealthy friends of her dead parents, and was universally considered to be a beautiful, intelligent and talented young lady. Jane kindly paid frequent visits to her aunt's humble home in Highbury.

Emma was out walking one morning, and determined to call upon Miss Bates. 'So kind of you to call in, Miss Woodhouse – our dear Jane is here – she wrote a long letter telling me she would come – always so considerate to

her poor aunt – she is so pleased to see you, aren't you Jane? – we are honoured by your visit – Jane is to stay for three months – she is suffering from a slight cold, isn't that so, Jane? – I really must collect some medicine – Mr Perry the pharmacist says that colds are terrible this year – Mrs Gilbert has a terrible chill which she caught off her housemaid – they have a housemaid now, you know.'

Emma smiled politely. Jane smiled respectfully.

'I find Jane so terribly reserved,' Emma confided in Mr Knightley that evening.

'That is a pity,' replied Mr Knightley. 'Jane Fairfax's excellent nature and superior talents should make her a natural friend for you. She needs a friend, Emma, and I always feel that you are negligent in your attentions towards her. Her friendship would do you more good than that of Harriet Smith.'

Emma felt ashamed. She knew that Mr Knightley was right, and that she should extend more warmth towards Jane. However, she was not happy that Mr Knightley assumed that Jane Fairfax would do her good. In fact, she was not at all happy with the extent of Mr Knightley's admiration for Jane Fairfax. She decided to change the subject. 'Frank Churchill is to arrive on Friday.'

'Hmpppph.' Mr Knightley looked displeased. 'I expect to find him a foolish, inconsiderate young man.'

Emma was surprised. Mr Knightley was usually very fair in his opinions. Such prejudice was most unlike him.

Have you made any clever guesses, Cassandra? Remember, I warned you that you might guess twenty things without guessing correctly.

Friday came, bringing with it Frank Churchill. Handsome and charming, and appearing particularly interested in becoming acquainted with Emma, he fulfilled all her expectations. Emma immediately liked him. By praising Highbury and his father's new wife, Frank soon made himself very agreeable to everybody.

Only Mr Knightley remained unimpressed. A few days after his arrival, Frank decided to go

all the way to London just to have his hair cut. Mr Woodhouse thought the journey too dangerous. Mr Knightley thought it vain, extravagant, and inconsiderate. 'He is just as foolish as I expected,' he muttered. Emma, on the other hand, noticed that after only two meetings she felt very comfortable with Frank Churchill.

Frank's lively spirits brought new energy to Highbury. Mrs Weston introduced him to all the important local people, and he was soon planning a village ball. 'Is there a family here by the name of Bates?' he asked Mr Woodhouse.

'Why, yes, dear Miss Bates. You must visit her.'

'I shall go immediately,' said Frank, rising from his chair. 'I was slightly acquainted with Miss Bates' niece, Miss Fairfax, when I was in Weymouth. I should pay my respects.'

'What a happy coincidence!' exclaimed Emma. 'You will find Jane Fairfax at Miss Bates' home now.'

Frank didn't look as surprised as Emma expected. She couldn't resist whispering, 'It is unlikely, however, that you will be able to talk to her, as her aunt never holds her tongue long enough for anyone else to speak.'

'Will I find Miss Fairfax well?'

'I am afraid that she is very unwell,' said Mr Woodhouse. Frank looked alarmed.

'No, no,' Emma reassured him. 'She has a very particular beauty, which gives her skin a rare softness and delicacy. It is not ill-health.'

'Indeed,' Frank smiled, recovering himself. 'If I remember correctly Miss Fairfax is naturally so pale that she always looks ill.'

He hurried away to pay his regards to Miss Bates and her niece.

Emma has always sworn that she will never marry. Do you think Frank Churchill could be the man to change her mind?

The following evening, Emma had another opportunity of seeing Frank Churchill when they were all invited to dine at a neighbour's house. She was pleased when Frank took a seat next to hers.

'I feel so happy here in Highbury,' he told her. 'The area, the climate, and ... ' he smiled at Emma, '... the people, all make it feel like home to me already.'

Emma smiled too. It was clear that Frank Churchill admired her. If he was not already in love with her, he showed signs of being very near it. It was probably only her own lack of encouragement that was holding him back. She turned to see Frank looking intently across the room to where Jane Fairfax was talking to Mr Knightley.

'Miss Fairfax does her hair in so odd a way,' Frank observed. 'Those strange curls – I cannot keep my eyes from her.'

A bustle seemed to surround Miss Bates and Jane Fairfax. Miss Bates' excited voice could easily be heard. 'A piano – a very good piano – arrived this morning – no, we don't know who sent it – it is all such a mystery –

Jane is quite at a loss – she plays it so beautifully – only yesterday Mr Knightley said what a pity it is that Jane has no instrument – a wonderful piano – all the way from London.'

Emma was intrigued by the news. Somebody had sent Jane Fairfax the gift of a piano. She must have a secret admirer, or perhaps a secret attachment. Emma smiled. Could the upright, reserved Jane Fairfax have a shameful secret?

'Why do you smile?' asked Frank.

'This must surely be an offering of love,' she whispered.

'Do you think so? Well, I shall suspect whatever you suspect.' In a louder voice, he added, 'Yes, only true affection could have prompted such a gift.'

Although Jane was embarrassed by all the fuss, she gave a secret smile of delight when she heard Frank's comment. Emma noticed with glee. Who could the admirer be?

Emma's enjoyment of the evening was tempered only by Mr Knightley's lack of spirits. She did not like to see him so unsociable, and was concerned when he left early. However, when Frank engaged her for the first two dances at the forthcoming ball, all thoughts of Mr Knightley were quite forgotten.

Dear Cassandra, I would dearly love to know what you are guessing at the moment. Please write and tell me.

The following morning brought disappointment. Frank Churchill had gone. Apparently his aunt was ill, and he had to be with her. He did not know when he would be able to return. The ball was cancelled, and Emma lost the opportunity of dancing with Frank.

Her spirits depressed by this unexpected loss, Emma examined her heart carefully. She felt that she must be in love, but could not decide how much.

As the weeks passed, Emma noticed with surprise that she was not miserable in Frank's absence, and was perfectly able to continue her usual activities. 'Why,' she thought, 'although he is undoubtedly in love with me, I am no longer in love with him. I hope that the distance between us will reduce his love for me.'

Emma now found more time for Harriet, who was still suffering from the heartbreak caused by Mr Elton. Emma was anxious for her friend, and wondered whether, on Frank's return, he might make a match for Harriet – once he got over his disappointment at her own indifference. However, she had learned her lesson, and had no intention of doing anything to bring them together.

Emma was therefore astonished and delighted to discover, two months after Frank's departure, that the two people in question had taken their first tentative steps towards true love without her interference. She looked out of her window one afternoon to see Harriet, trembling and tearful, leaning heavily upon the supporting arm of none other than Frank Churchill.

'Oh, Miss Woodhouse,' gasped Harriet, before fainting into Frank's arms. A fainting lady needs reviving, and an explanation must be given. On her way to visit Emma, Harriet had been followed by some gypsy children. As they chased her, she had fallen. Who knows what might have become of her had not Frank Churchill, who was at last returning to Hartfield, arrived on the scene and chased the gypsies away?

'A fine young man and a lovely young woman thrown together in such circumstances must clearly be affected,' mused Emma that evening. Although many might consider Harriet somewhat beneath Frank Churchill, stranger things had happened.

This is becoming quite a complicated puzzle now, don't you think? I wonder whether you have any idea how it will all be resolved?

Frank's return meant that the long-awaited ball could now take place. Emma was relieved to sense that his love for her had faded into friendship and, when he reminded her of her engagement to open the dancing with him, she accepted as a friend. When the second dance began, Emma noticed Harriet sitting alone, whilst Mrs Weston talked to Mr Elton nearby.

'Do you not dance, Mr Elton?' asked Mrs Weston kindly.

'Certainly, if you will dance with me,' bowed the gentleman.

'Me! Oh no, I meant a much better dancer. Miss Smith is without a partner. I should like to see her on the dance floor.'

'Miss Smith! Oh ... I had not noticed. No – I do not think I will dance.'

Mrs Weston was stunned by his rudeness. Seeing that poor Harriet had overheard the conversation, Emma felt her pain.

A moment later, however, Harriet was all smiles. Mr Knightley, who rarely danced, was leading her onto the dance floor. Emma caught his eye with a look of warm gratitude. His dancing proved to be excellent, and Emma could barely take her eyes off him as he guided the bounding Harriet around the room.

When the dance ended, Emma went straight to thank Mr Knightley.

'Mr Elton's rudeness was unpardonable,' he observed. 'Why should he want to wound Harriet?'

Emma remained quiet. Mr Knightley gently took her hand. 'Who will you dance with next?' he asked.

'You, if you will ask me.'

'I am no longer in love with Mr Elton,' Harriet announced one morning as she sat with Emma. 'He who now occupies my thoughts is far superior to Mr Elton. Such a gentleman. I would not presume to hope, but yet there are signs. I was in such distress and then I saw him, and he rescued me. I was so grateful. Now, when I see him I cannot imagine that I ever loved Mr Elton.' Emma understood Harriet's meaning precisely, and felt that Harriet's signs of affection for Frank were sufficiently encouraging to need no active help from her.

A few days later, the weather being fine,
an outing to Box Hill, a local picnic spot, was
arranged. Emma walked with Mrs Weston
towards the spot chosen for lunch. 'Emma, I have
been following your example, and I believe I have
made a match,' said Mrs Weston conspiratorially.

Emma was interested.

'What do you say to Mr Knightley and Jane
Fairfax?'

'It cannot be!' exclaimed Emma. She looked
ahead to where Mr Knightley was walking with
Jane. His praise of Jane had indeed always been
very warm. Emma felt uncomfortable.

Mrs Weston continued. 'I think it was he who sent the piano. He loves to hear her play.'

Emma had to acknowledge the logic in this, but did not think that sending a mystery present was Mr Knightley's style. She walked away in troubled silence.

A little later, Emma was astonished to find Mr Knightley himself by her side. He seemed quiet and concerned. After a short silence, he said gently, 'Emma, have you any reason to suspect an attachment between Jane Fairfax and Frank Churchill?' Emma laughed in astonishment.

'I think I have seen signs of a private understanding between them,' he continued.

'Mr Knightley, leave matchmaking to me. You are mistaken. They are as far away from an attachment as any two people can be. I am confident of Frank's indifference. I see more signs of your admiration for Jane than of his.'

'Oh, so you have settled that I should marry Miss Fairfax, have you? Well, yes – anybody may know how highly I think of her.' Emma forced herself to remain silent. 'But she has not the liveliness of spirit which a man would wish for in a wife.' Seeming irritated, he walked away.

During the picnic, Emma noticed that Mr Knightley seemed to be observing her. She tried to make him smile, but he looked grave. She was relieved to find Frank, by contrast, in high spirits. It seemed that all that he cared about was to amuse her. She gave him friendly encouragement. She was aware that it might look like flirtation, but she was now confident that Frank was no longer in love with her.

'They are all so quiet, particularly Miss Fairfax,' complained Frank loudly. Jane looked displeased.

Frank gained everyone's attention by clearing his throat loudly. Then he announced: 'Miss Woodhouse would like each one of you to say three things to entertain the group.'

Mr Knightley frowned. Jane stood up and walked away.

'Oh dear,' laughed Miss Bates, 'I shall be sure to say three dull things as soon as I open my mouth.'

'Pardon me, Miss Bates,' Emma smiled, 'but please note that you are limited – only three!'

Everybody fell silent. Miss Bates blushed. 'Oh dear, yes, I am sorry,' she stammered. 'I will try to hold my tongue.'

Mr Knightley looked at Emma gravely. Emma immediately understood the pain she had so carelessly caused.

'Emma, that was badly done,' said Mr Knightley as he helped her into her carriage at the end of the day. 'How could you be so unfeeling?'

Finally, alone in her carriage, Emma wept tears of confusion and shame. How could she make it up to poor Miss Bates? How could she regain Mr Knightley's good opinion?

Poor Emma. What does she know of other people's hearts? What does she know of her own? Have you discovered the secrets of any of my characters' hearts?

The following morning, Emma went immediately to apologise to Miss Bates. Upon her return, she found an anxious Mrs Weston waiting for her. 'Oh, Emma, it is the most surprising business. Frank has confessed it this morning.' Emma was intrigued. 'He has announced an attachment!' Emma immediately thought of Harriet. 'No, more than an attachment. A secret engagement! He and Jane Fairfax have been engaged since they first met in Weymouth.'

'Good god! You are not serious?'

So, Mr Knightley was right. Had you foreseen this, Cassandra? There have been several clues.

Emma's shock made Mrs Weston anxious. She was afraid that Emma herself was in love with Frank. Emma immediately reassured her that her love had long since passed. 'However, I am stunned by the dishonesty of them both: coming to Highbury with such a secret between them.'

Frank had told his father that the secrecy had been necessary because he feared opposition to the match from his aunt. However, Jane had felt such displeasure and frustration on the day of the Box Hill picnic as she watched Frank's behaviour with Emma, that she had felt impelled to end the engagement. This had forced his hand. Frank, who was deeply in love with Jane, had now decided to end the secrecy.

How was Emma going to break the news to Harriet?

'How odd,' was all that Harriet said when Emma told her the news.

'Harriet, how can you remain so calm?' Emma was astonished.

Harriet looked confused. Then she blushed. 'You do not think that I care about Mr Churchill? Oh no, I am thinking of somebody far superior to Frank.'

'But did you not say ... ? Who were you speaking of when ... ?' Emma stopped, suddenly understanding her friend. 'You couldn't be ... are you in love with Mr Knightley?'

'Indeed,' said Harriet quietly. 'Ever since he rescued me at the ball I have thought of no one else. At first I thought only to admire from afar, but now I think he might love me.'

Emma could not speak. At last she knew her own heart. Mr Knightley must marry no one but Emma Woodhouse.

Oh, the blunders and the blindness of her own head and heart! Why had she never compared Frank with Mr Knightley? Why had she never realised why Mr Knightley's good opinion of her mattered so much? If only Harriet had married Robert Martin months ago!

Emma stopped and collected herself. She looked at poor Harriet, who was anxious for encouragement. This is all my fault, reflected Emma. If Harriet, from being humble, has grown vain, it is my doing. The possibility of Harriet becoming mistress in Mr Knightley's home was unbearable and yet, she now believed, it was indeed a possibility.

'Dear Harriet, I admire your choice, but I am unable to encourage you. You must watch him carefully for any signs of affection.'

'I have done so, Miss Woodhouse, and I am certain that I see them.'

Emma felt the beginnings of a headache, and asked Harriet to leave. Finally alone, the tears fell as she remembered all her foolish schemes. If only she had listened to wise, gentle, kind Mr Knightley.

Dear Cassandra, our puzzles are drawing towards an end. Jane is to marry Frank and, it seems, Harriet has received encouragement from Mr Knightley. Emma always said she would never marry, and now she seems likely to fulfil this vow against her own wishes.

The following morning, in need of fresh air, Emma decided to take a walk in the grounds of Hartfield. The cool breeze lifted her spirits. Refreshed, she turned back towards the house, only to see none other than Mr Knightley walking towards her.

She gasped. After a polite greeting, they walked together in silence. He seemed to be trying to look at her face. Emma felt a sense of dread. She knew that he wanted to ask her about Harriet.

'Emma,' he began, 'I have heard the news about Frank and Miss Fairfax. His behaviour towards you has been unpardonable. I can only hope that time, my dearest Emma, will heal your wound.' He took her arm in his.

'I have many things to regret,' smiled Emma, 'but loving Frank is not one of them. I thought myself in love at first, but know now that I was mistaken.'

'Emma,' said Mr Knightley with eagerness, 'are you then really free of affection?'

'Please believe that I have long been free of affection for Frank Churchill. I wish him and Jane well.

I believe them sincerely in love.'

Mr Knightley fell silent again. Emma trembled. 'Emma, I must speak. I must tell you something, although I may regret it.'

Emma desperately wanted him to stay silent, but he looked so anxious, so unhappy, that she had to listen, whatever pain it might cause her. 'Speak to me as a friend,' she invited him.

'As a friend!' Mr Knightley stopped and looked into her eyes. His expression overpowered her. 'If I loved you less, I might be able to talk about it more easily, but I have loved you for a long, long time.'

In a flutter of spirits such as she had never known, Emma was at a loss for words. They looked, they smiled, and then they spoke together about the years of happiness that lay ahead of them. They walked for a long time in the garden, discussing all the puzzles of the last year.

The only cloud on Emma's bright horizon was the prospect of breaking the news to her father, and to Harriet.

Dear Cassandra,

Thank you for writing that you have grown to like Emma Woodhouse. I thought you would eventually. You know, so concerned was she for her father's happiness that she was prepared to wait until his death before she married Mr Knightley. Mr Knightley, however, found a solution. He would live with his wife at Hartfield until such a time as they might put their own comfort first.

And so, our story is almost at an end. Has anything surprised you, or did you see the end right from the beginning? Well, here is a final event that might surprise you. Poor Harriet was at first heartbroken, but within months she herself was married. Yes – Robert Martin once again proposed to her. This time he was accepted.

We must believe them happy for, although Harriet might have appeared to be in love several times in the course of our story, her affection for her first love was readily renewed.

In an edition of Shakespeare in the library at Hartfield, somebody has highlighted the line, 'The course of true love never did run smooth.' How very true that is.

Yours affectionately,

Jane

TAKING THINGS FURTHER

The real read

This *Real Read* version of *Emma* is a retelling of Jane Austen's magnificent work. If you would like to read the full novel in all its original splendour, many complete editions are available, from bargain paperbacks to beautifully-bound hardbacks. You may well find a copy in your local charity shop.

Filling in the spaces

The loss of so many of Jane Austen's original words is a sad but necessary part of the shortening process. We have had to make some difficult decisions, omitting subplots and details, some important, some less so, but all interesting. We have also, at times, taken the liberty of combining two events into one, or of giving a character words or actions that originally belong to another. The points below will fill in some of the gaps, but nothing can beat the original.

- Jane Austen's *Emma* does not contain letters to Jane's sister Cassandra, although Jane did mention the novel in her letters and did suggest that nobody would like the heroine.

- Emma's sister, Isabella, is married to Mr Knightley's brother. They live in London with their children. Both Emma and Mr Knightley are very fond of their nephews.

- Miss Bates lives with her elderly mother. They struggle to 'make a small income go a long way'.

- Jane Fairfax, an orphan, has been raised as a second daughter by Colonel Campbell. Emma suspects her of secretly loving the colonel's son-in-law, Mr Dixon.

- Emma suspects that Mr Dixon sent the piano. She shares her thoughts with Frank.

- Jane has no independent income, and is destined to become a governess.

- Mr and Mrs Weston secretly hope that Emma will marry Frank.

- Frank Churchill's visit to his father is postponed several times. He always blames his aunt's moods and ill-health.

- In contrast to Frank, Jane dutifully decides to spend her last few months of freedom before she becomes a governess visiting her aunt and grandmother.

- Mr Knightley criticises Emma for her lack of application to improving her talents. His admiration for Jane's superior accomplishments therefore irritates Emma.

- Mr Elton marries a Miss Hawkins. She and Emma dislike each other immediately.

- The recently-married Mrs Elton dominates Jane Fairfax. This irritates Frank.

- Frank Churchill is only free to marry Jane Fairfax after the death of his aunt, who would never have allowed it.

- Jane Austen gives several hints about Mr Knightley's true feelings for Emma, as well as those of Frank and Jane.

- Frank and Jane are forgiven by everybody for keeping their engagement a secret. Everybody wishes them well.

Back in time

Jane Austen began writing *Emma* in 1814. It was published in 1816, just one year before her death at the age of forty-one.

A keen letter writer, Jane Austen maintained a regular correspondence with her older sister, Cassandra. This *Real Reads Emma* draws upon the idea of the letters, rather than upon the contents of the letters themselves.

At the same time as writing *Emma*, Jane Austen was advising her niece Anna upon the techniques of writing a novel. She wrote, 'three or four families in a country village is the very thing to work on'. She follows her own advice in *Emma*. Through writing about something that seems so simple, Jane Austen creates a complex novel, revealing the interaction and interdependence of Highbury's small community.

Due to her father's personality, Emma has never been far from Highbury. Even for a woman of her financial security and independence, Emma's activities are still influenced by the men around her.

In all of her novels, Jane Austen shows the restrictions within which women lived. As a woman, Miss Bates did not inherit her family's wealth. To avoid her aunt's fate, Jane Fairfax must either become a governess or marry wisely. Emma seeks to improve Harriet's future by arranging an advantageous marriage. However, Jane Austen would never have advised anybody to marry without love.

Finding out more

We recommend the following books and websites to gain a greater understanding of Jane Austen's England:

Books

- Gill Hornby, *Who was Jane Austen? The Girl with the Magic Pen*, Short Books, 2005.

- Jon Spence, *Becoming Jane Austen*, Hambledon Continuum, 2007.

- Henrietta Webb and Josephine Ross, *Jane Austen's Guide to Good Manners: Compliments, Charades and Horrible Blunders*, Bloomsbury Publishing, 2006.

- Dominique Enwright, *The Wicked Wit of Jane Austen*, Michael O'Mara, 2007.

- Lauren Henderson, *Jane Austen's Guide to Romance: The Regency Rules*, Headline, 2007.

- Deirdre Le Faye, *Jane Austen: The World of Her Novels*, Frances Lincoln, 2003.

- Tom Tierney, *Fashions of the Regency Period Paper Dolls*, Dover, 2000.

- Emma Campbell Webster, *Lost in Austen: Create Your Own Jane Austen Adventure*, Riverhead, 2007.

Websites

- www.janeausten.co.uk
Home of the Jane Austen Centre in Bath, England.

- www.janeaustensoci.freeuk.com
Home of the Jane Austen Society. Includes summaries of, and brief commentaries on, her novels.

- www.pemberley.com
A very enthusiastic site for Jane Austen enthusiasts.

- www.literaryhistory.com/19thC/AUSTEN
A selective and helpful guide to links to other Jane Austen sites.

Films

- *Emma* (1996), adapted and directed by Andrew Davies, ITV.

- *Emma* (1996), adapted and directed by Douglas McGrath, Disney.

- *Clueless* (2000), adapted and directed by Amy Heckerling, Paramount.

Food for thought

Here are some things to think about if you are reading *Emma* alone, or ideas for discussion if you are reading it with friends.

In retelling *Emma* we have tried to recreate, as accurately as possible, Jane Austen's original plot and characters. We have also tried to imitate aspects of her style. Remember, however, that this is not the original work; thinking about the points below, therefore, can help you begin to understand Jane Austen's craft. To move forward from here, turn to the full-length version of *Emma* and lose yourself in her wonderful portrayals of human nature.

Starting points

- Which character interests you the most? Why?

- What do you think of Emma? Do your feelings towards her change as you read on? How?

- Did you solve any of the 'puzzles' before Emma? Choose one of the relationships and find as many clues as you can.

- Consider the differences between Frank Churchill and Mr Knightley.

- Consider Emma's friendship with Harriet Smith. Why does Mr Knightley think Jane would be a better friend for Emma?

- At the end of the novel which of the couples do you feel has the best chance of being happy? Why?

Themes

What do you think Jane Austen is saying about the following themes in *Emma*?

- friendship

- the relationship between wealth, social status and marriage

- women in society

- social respect and politeness

Style

Can you find paragraphs containing examples of the following?

- a person exposing their true character through something they say or the way they speak

- humour

- the writer allowing the reader to know more than the characters know

- the use of letters to progress the plot

Look closely at how these paragraphs are written. What do you notice? Can you write a paragraph in the same style?